Dr. Jon Jon Saves the Moon

Jackson Apollo Mancini

Illustrated by Arielle Trenk

BEYOND WORDS

Portland, Oregon

I dedicate this book to
the real Dr. Jon Jon, Dr. Jon Hattenhauer,
for letting me believe you were a real moon doctor.

BEYOND WORDS
1750 S.W. Skyline Blvd., Suite 20
Portland, Oregon 97221-2543
503–531–8700/503-531-8773 fax
www.beyondword.com

Managing Editor: Lindsay S. Easterbrooks-Brown
Editor: Michele Cohn
Illustrations: Arielle Trenk
Design: Sara E. Blum

The text of this book was set in Bembo Std.

The illustrations for this book were rendered in Adobe Photoshop.

This first Beyond Words hardcover edition March 2021
Beyond Words Publishing is an imprint of Simon & Schuster, Inc.
and the Beyond Words logo is a registered trademark of Beyond Words Publishing, Inc.

For more information about special discounts for bulk purchases,
please contact Beyond Words Special Sales at 503–531–8700 or specialsales@beyondword.com.

Manufactured in Korea

10 9 8 7 6 5 4 3 2 1

Library of Congress Control Number: 2020948840

ISBN 978-1-58270-761-7

The corporate mission of Beyond Words Publishing, Inc.:
Inspire to Integrity

Since the beginning of time kids have looked up at the night sky to gaze at the glowing white moon and bright twinkling stars.

But slowly, over time, the moon started to look a little bit different.

Until one day the kids looked up and saw that the moon had turned green.

At first the kids were confused. They wondered: When was the last time the moon had glowed white? They began to worry. What could be making the moon green? Could the moon be sick?

Adults began to meet all over the planet to discuss what could be done to help the moon. But no one quite knew where to start.

That was until one little boy
stepped forward and said to the adults,
"We need a moon doctor!"

"A moon doctor?" the people asked.
Did Earth have a moon doctor?

There was only one place to check—NASA!

There they found Dr. Jon Jon, who assured them that he could in fact give the moon a checkup.

So, it was decided that Dr. Jon Jon would travel to the moon in a rocket ship, and with stethoscope in hand, he set out.

The kids back on Earth held their breath and crossed their fingers as they watched Dr. Jon Jon's flight to the moon. Hopefully he could help the moon feel better.

But once Dr. Jon Jon landed on the moon, he was really confused.

The moon looked . . . *Ok*.

After looking around a little bit he explained to his patient that the people on Earth were very worried about the moon's health.

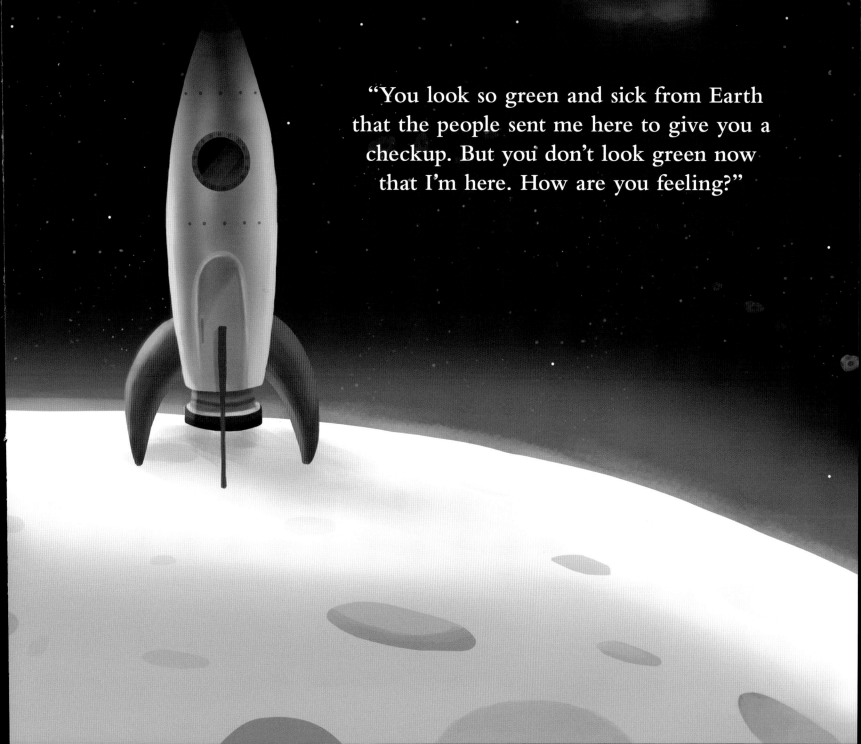

"You look so green and sick from Earth that the people sent me here to give you a checkup. But you don't look green now that I'm here. How are you feeling?"

The moon thought for a moment and then answered,

"As you can see, I'm not sick, but I do feel sad. I look green from the surface of the planet because my friend the Earth is actually sick. What they see when they look at me is how the Earth feels.

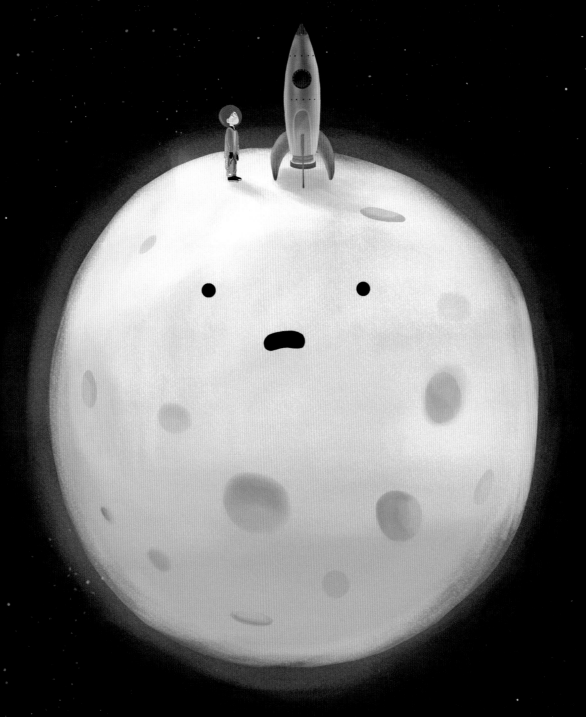

The people down on Earth's surface have forgotten how to take care of their home. They throw garbage on the ground, and that garbage ends up in the forests, rivers, and oceans. It makes the animals sick. It makes the land and the water sick. The people cut down trees, but don't plant new ones to replace them. They build their cities and towns on land that belongs to the animals."

"But, what can we do?" asked Dr. Jon Jon.

"It took a long time for the Earth to get sick,"
the moon answered.

"It will take a long time for it to get better again.

But if you all work hard together you can help the Earth."

And so the moon told Dr. Jon Jon just how the adults and kids down on Earth could help the planet start to feel better.

After a high five with the moon and a promise to visit again soon, Dr. Jon Jon got into his rocket ship and set off back to the surface of the Earth.

When Dr. Jon Jon got back to Earth, the children ran to greet him. They couldn't wait to hear what he had learned.

Dr. Jon Jon excitedly shared what the moon had told him during the checkup.

At first the people were confused, but as they looked around, they started to see what the moon was talking about.

There were pieces of garbage along the sides of the road. There were lots of places that they could plant more trees. And there weren't as many animals around as there had been before the city was built.

Dr. Jon Jon explained how each person could help the Earth feel better by making sure their garbage was thrown away properly, and by reusing and recycling things instead of throwing them away in the first place.

Dr. Jon Jon told the people that for the Earth
to feel better, the planet needed all the animals
and ocean creatures to be healthy and happy.
The moon had told him that all the people of
Earth must always try to give the creatures of
the land and sea a nice clean place to live.

Dr. Jon Jon asked everyone to work together as a team, because we all must share this planet as our home.

The Earth wasn't made better overnight. The people started to work together to change their ways and to clean up the oceans and lands. Overtime, when the people on Earth looked up at the night sky, the moon started to look a little bit better. A little more like its old self.

And Dr. Jon Jon kept his promise to visit the moon and check up on how the moon was feeling. They became good friends.

Acknowledgments

I want to thank the team at Beyond Words Publishing for helping me make my book. I want to also thank Arielle Trenk for drawing the pictures. Finally, thank you to all the kids working to save our planet.

Kid Resources

Interested in how you can help the planet Earth feel better? Here are some great websites just for kids like you who want to help make their home the best it can be!

National Geographic offers lots of fun stories, photos, interactive games, and more to get you inspired in helping the planet.
- https://kids.nationalgeographic.com/
- https://www.nationalgeographic.com/family/

PBS Kids offers videos, games, and so many cute baby animals to learn about—there's even the Wild Kratts interactive website!
- https://pbskids.org/
- https://pbskids.org/wildkratts/

National Institute of Environmental Health and Sciences has a great "discover, explore, learn" website just for kids.
- https://kids.niehs.nih.gov/

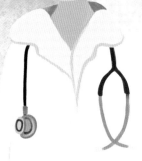

NASA Climate Kids is a website all about looking at our planet from space and how kids can work to fix the many injuries the Earth suffers.
- https://climatekids.nasa.gov/